IT'S APRIL FOOLS' DAY!

by STEVEN KROLL

illustrated by JENI BASSETT

SCHOLASTIC INC.
New York Toronto London Auckland Sydney

ISBN 0-590-44348-8

Text copyright © 1990 Steven Kroll.
Illustrations copyright © 1990 by Jeni Bassett.
All rights reserved. Published by Scholastic Inc.,
730 Broadway, New York, NY 10003, by arrangement with
Holiday House.

12 11 10 9 8 7 6 5 4 3   3 4 5 6/9

Printed in the U.S.A.   24

First Scholastic printing, March 1991

For my nephew Lincoln Anderson,
child of April Fools' Day

S.K.

On April Fools' Day, Alice was scared to leave the house. She knew Horace the Bully would be waiting for her outside.

Finally, she opened the door a crack and peered around it.

No Horace.

She walked down the front steps and looked around.

No Horace.

She marched right up to the front gate and flung it open. SPLASH! A pail of water fell on her head.

"Oh, Horace!" wailed Alice as the water dripped over her ears and wet her whiskers. "You are *so* mean!"

"I like being mean," said Horace. "April Fool, Alice!"

Alice shook herself dry. Then she decided to go for a walk. She had gone only a little way when she thought she heard Horace whisper, "Psst, Alice, I've got something for you."

Alice froze.

Horace leaped out from behind a tree and pulled her tail.

Then he chased her around the block until she hid under a bush.
"April Fool, Alice!" she heard him screech.

"Oh, Horace," said Alice, "why are you picking on me? Don't you have any friends?"

"Nooooo," said Horace. "Only you, Alice."

"I'm not your friend. Don't you have brothers and sisters?"

"Nope. Not one. You can be my sister if you want."

"I don't want to be your sister. Not when you're so terrible."

"I like being terrible," said Horace.

Alice crept back to her house. She sat down to think in her favorite chair.

Poppa Cat came into the room. "Why don't you go out and get some exercise," he said. "It's a lovely day."

"I can't," said Alice. "Horace is out there. It's April Fools' Day, and he's playing mean tricks on me."

"That's not very nice," said Poppa Cat. "Let me talk to him."

Poppa Cat went outside. There was Horace, leaning against the gate.

When he saw Poppa Cat, he grinned. "Hello, sir," he said. "How are you today?"

"Just fine, Horace," said Poppa Cat. "What's this I hear about your playing mean tricks on Alice?"

"I don't play tricks. I just want to play. And she doesn't want to play with me."

"I'll talk to her," said Poppa Cat.

He went back inside. "Alice," he said, "Horace says all he wants to do is play. Why don't you go out and join him?"

"He just wants to play?" said Alice.

"That's what he said," said Poppa Cat.

Carefully, Alice opened the front door. Carefully, she crept down the steps and through the gate. Horace was waiting. He yanked her tail!

Then he chased her around the block until she hid under a bush.

"Oh, Horace," she said. "You are so bad!"

"I like being bad!" said Horace.

At that moment, Alice decided she had had enough. She sneaked back to the house. On the way, she thought about all the terrible things she could do to Horace. She hoped he'd stay away long enough for her to get the front yard ready.

"Horace," she called an hour later, "Horace, are you there?"

"Of course I'm here," said Horace from the other side of the gate. "Why haven't you come out to play?"

"Because I've been thinking about you, Horace, and I've been making an extra special surprise."

"What do you mean, surprise?"

"Come and find out. It's all ready."

Horace opened the gate. The bucket of water sitting on top fell on his head.

"April Fool!" yelled Alice.

"What the—?" gasped Horace, stepping smack into the mousetrap Alice had placed in just the right spot.

"April Fool!" cried Alice.

"Owwwww!" yelled Horace, grabbing the mousetrap.

But the mousetrap was attached to a string, and the string was attached to the branch of a tree. As Horace grabbed the mousetrap, the branch dipped and an orange fell on his head.

"Ouch!" said Horace, and sat down hard.

"April Fool!" shouted Alice.

When Horace had stopped feeling dizzy, he removed the bucket from his head and the mousetrap from his paw. He looked up at Alice.

"Hmmph," he said. "Some trick."

"Yeah," said Alice. "I thought so, too."

"You're pretty good at tricks. You really could be my friend."

"No, thanks," said Alice.

"Who's the mean one now?" said Horace. He turned and walked through the gate, slamming it behind him.

All through lunch, Alice worried about Horace. She was sure he'd do something to get back at her. She was so worried, she could hardly eat her Frisky Vittles.

After lunch, Alice took a catnap in the laundry basket. Maybe she would just nap all afternoon. Maybe Horace would forget about her.

An hour went by. Then the doorbell rang. Alice went to answer it.

Horace was standing on the front steps. Quickly he held out a bunch of tulips.

"I'm sorry," he said. "I'm through with being a bully. Will you come out and play?"

"Will you promise not to pull my tail? said Alice.
"I promise."
"Or dump water on me?"
"I promise."
"Or chase me under the bush?"
"I promise."
"Then I'll come play," said Alice.

They walked for a little while. Then Horace said, "Look at that big tree. Why don't we climb it?"

They climbed up. Then they played hide-and-seek in the branches and ran down the trunk.

"Whew," said Alice, catching her breath, "that really was fun. And now, Horace, I'm going to pull your tail and chase you around the block!"

Alice chased Horace.

"April Fool!" she giggled, as she pounced on him.

Then Horace chased Alice.
"April Fool!" he shouted.
They ended up tumbling on the grass.

"No more April Fools!" said Alice.
"No more April Fools!" said Horace.
"Only happy times," said Alice.
"Only happy times," said Horace.
From then on, they were the best of friends.